(B)

$\left(h - \ldots \right)$

$\sqrt{5}$

(B)

(13)

$m\angle(4) = \sqrt{3}$

$43 \cdot Ad \neq (c$

$H \pm D(E) \neq I \, (c) D = -4 \, (c)$

$\text{OC} I$

$\theta = B < O$

Illustrations by Isabel Muñoz.

Written by Jane Kent.

Designed by Nick Ackland.

WHITE STAR KIDS

White Star Kids® is a registered trademark property of White Star s.r.l.

© 2019 White Star s.r.l.
Piazzale Luigi Cadorna, 6
20123 Milan, Italy
www.whitestar.it

Produced by i am a bookworm.

ISBN 978-88-544-1362-7
1 2 3 4 5 6   23 22 21 20 19

Printed in Turkey

The life of Stephen Hawking

WSkids
WHITE STAR KIDS

My name is Stephen Hawking and I am a world-famous scientist and author. I'm known not only for my work on black holes and relativity, but because I beat the odds and lived with a form of Motor Neuron Disease for years longer than doctors predicted.

Let me tell you my life story and show you how I didn't let disability stop me from following my dreams.

I was born in Oxford on 8th January 1942. I always loved that this date was also the 300th anniversary of the death of Italian astronomer and mathematician, Galileo Galilei. My parents were Frank and Isobel Hawking and I was their first child. They went on the have two girls, Mary and Philippa, and when I was fourteen years old they adopted another child, Edward.

Frank

Isobel

Me

Philippa

Mary

People described our family as "eccentric" and "thinkers". We often ate in silence while reading books, we kept bees in our basement and our family car was a converted London taxi.

My father was a researcher in the area of tropical medicine. He wanted me to follow in his footsteps and also go into medicine, but I preferred mathematics. I went to St. Albans School at the age of eleven and although I was bright, activities outside the classroom held my attention more than my lessons did.

I had a few close friends and we loved playing board games together, as well as making up our own. Once we even built our own computer from recycled parts and used it to solve math problems. But my favorite pastime was lying on the grass in our garden with my mother and siblings, gazing up at the stars in the night sky.

I started at University College, Oxford, in 1959 at the age of 17.
It was the same college that my father had attended.
Math was not an available course there and so I studied Physics
instead, with a particular focus on Cosmology.

As with school, I didn't put a lot of effort into my university studies. Thankfully I was intelligent enough to get away with not doing much work and at the end of three years, I earned a first class honors degree in Natural Science.

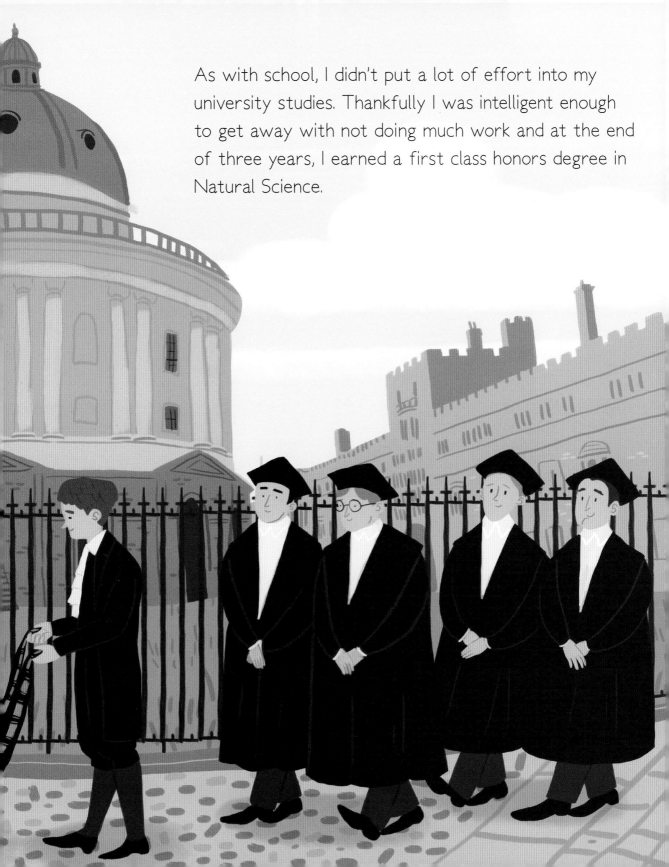

In 1962 I went on to study for a PhD in Cosmology at Trinity Hall, Cambridge University. It was during my first year there, shortly after my 21st birthday in 1963, that I was diagnosed with amyotrophic lateral sclerosis - or ALS - which is a form of Motor Neuron Disease. It meant that the nerves controlling my muscles were shutting down.

I had first begun to have health problems while I was at Oxford. Sometimes I would trip over and my speech would be slurred. I tried to hide my symptoms, but eventually my father noticed and took me to see a doctor. Tests revealed I was in the early stages of ALS and doctors said I might only live for another two and a half years. But I was determined to fight it!

Just before my diagnosis, I had met a young lady called Jane Wilde at a New Year's party. She was studying languages at Westfield College, University of London. We quickly fell in love and she stood by me when I told her that I had ALS. We got engaged in 1964 and were married a year later.

We went on to have three children. Robert was born in 1967, Lucy in 1970 and finally Timothy in 1979.

Prior to my disease, I hadn't really put much effort into my studies. But knowing that I might not have long to live gave me the push I needed to focus on my work and finish my PhD. In 1966 I finally handed in my doctoral thesis, entitled "Properties of Expanding Universes". I went on to become a member of the Institute of Astronomy in Cambridge in 1968.

I was forced to start using a wheelchair the following year, as the ALS took hold. Within a couple of years I began to need assistance with many tasks and my speech was getting so slurred that people had difficulty understanding me.

I was fascinated by the work of Roger Penrose, a cosmologist whose findings on the fate of stars and the creation of black holes were groundbreaking. In 1974 I was able to show that black holes, which are made when stars collapse, don't swallow matter completely, as previously thought. In fact, some radiation can escape the gravitational force.

My theory made me something of a celebrity in the world of science and I became a fellow of the Royal Society that same year, at the age of 32. Penrose and I then began to work together to expand on our ideas and learn more about the creation of the universe.

In 1985 I caught pneumonia and had to have a tracheotomy, which meant I permanently lost my voice. I was worried that I would no longer be able to work, but a computer programmer from California called Walter Woltosz stepped in. He had developed the Equalizer, a speaking program whereby I could select words on a computer screen with a handheld clicker, which then passed through a speech synthesizer.

Eventually I was unable to use my hands, but thankfully the program could also be used through head or eye movement. So I switched to directing it via a cheek muscle that was attached to a sensor.

The computer program allowed me to continue to write. I worked on many scientific papers and also on several books that I hoped would bring my ideas to a wider audience. In 1988, "A Brief History of Time" was published, giving an overview of space and time, as well as reviewing the theories of great thinkers such as Newton and Einstein.

It proved extremely popular, selling millions of copies worldwide, being translated into more than 40 languages and spending more than four years at the top of the London Sunday Times' best-seller list.

In 1991, the Oscar-winning filmmaker Errol Morris created a documentary about my life. The title was "A Brief History of Time", the same as my book. I went onto appear in many popular TV shows, including "The Big Bang Theory" and "The Simpsons". This allowed me to reach a wider, often younger, audience and show off my wicked sense of humor, too! I became known as the rock-star scientist.

I visited Kennedy Space Center, Florida, in 2007 and while there, I was able to experience zero gravity. I boarded a modified Boeing 727 and flew for two hours over the Atlantic Ocean. When I was released from my wheelchair, I was completely weightless. Newspapers around the world printed photos of me floating in the air.

I appeared at a conference in Sweden in 2015, to discuss new theories around black holes. I talked about the issue, known as the "information paradox", of what becomes of an object when it enters a black hole, and proposed a new idea.

It was thought that information about an object disappeared forever once it crossed the outer boundary, or "event horizon", of a black hole. I suggested instead that the information about the object is stored within a surrounding "halo". I noted that black holes are not eternal prisons and perhaps the stored information could be released one day.

In late 2017, Cambridge University posted my doctoral thesis on its website. It was incredibly popular, so much so that overwhelming demand crashed the university server. By the end of the first day, it had been viewed over 60,000 times.

In my thesis I aimed to show that the Big Bang theory, in which the universe began from a single point, was possible. Although it is now an accepted scientific fact, when I wrote my thesis back in 1966 scientists were still arguing over the idea.

At the age of 76, I passed away on 14th March 2018 at my home in Cambridge. I had finally succumbed to ALS, having lived with the disease for over 50 years longer than expected.

That same month it was announced that my ashes would be placed in London's Westminster Abbey. I would rest alongside other scientific greats, such as Sir Isaac Newton and Charles Darwin.

I am thought of as the brightest star in science and my legacy will always live on. I hope that my spirit, determination and many, many triumphs in the face of adversity will be an inspiration to others who come up against their own trials. Life is a precious gift, so make the most of your time and never let anything dull your shine. No matter what setbacks you encounter, there is always a way to achieve your dreams - you just have to get out there and find it.

Hawking was born the 8th January in Oxford.

Just after his 21st birthday, Hawking was diagnosed with ALS, a form of Motor Neuron Disease.

At age 17, he started at University College, Oxford.

1942

1959

1963

1953

1962

He attended St. Albans School at the age of eleven.

Hawking completed his degree in Natural Science. He went on to study for a PhD in Cosmology at Trinity Hall, Cambridge University. He met Jane Wilde at a New Year's party.

They were
married.

His son Robert
was born.

1965

1967

1964

1966

1968

Hawking handed
in his doctoral
thesis.

Jane and Hawking
got engaged.

Hawking became a
member of the Institute
of Astronomy in
Cambridge.

Hawking released his
black hole radiation
theory and began
working with
cosmologist
Roger Penrose.

Hawking caught pneumonia and
had to have a tracheotomy.
Unable to speak, he began using
Walter Woltosz's computer
program to communicate.

He was forced
to start using a
wheelchair.

1969

1974

1985

1970

1979

His son Timothy
was born.

His daughter
Lucy was born.

Errol Morris's documentary, also called "A Brief History of Time", was released. Hawking began appearing on TV shows.

He talked about the black hole "information paradox" at a conference in Sweden.

1991

2015

1988

2007

2018

Hawking died on 14th March, aged 76.

A BRIEF HISTORY OF TIME
FROM THE BIG BANG TO BLACK HOLES
STEPHEN W.HAWKING
WITH AN INTRODUCTION BY CARL SAGAN

While visiting the Kennedy Space Center in Florida, Hawking experienced zero gravity.

His book, "A Brief History of Time", was published.

QUESTIONS

Q1. Hawking was born on the 300th anniversary of whose death?

_____

Q2. What did the Hawking family keep in their basement?

_____

Q3. Where did Hawking study for a PhD in cosmology?

_____

Q4. Who did Hawking meet at a New Year's party?

_____

Q5. What disease was Hawkin diagnosed with?

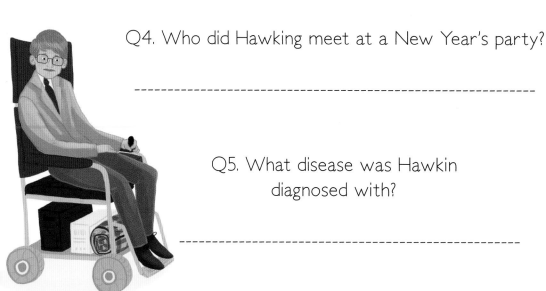

_____

Q6. What was the title of Hawking's
doctoral thesis?

Q7. Hawking worked with which cosmologist
to learn more about the creation of the universe?

Q8. How did Hawking speak through a computer?

Q9. When was Hawking's book, "A Brief
History of Time", published?

Q10. Where was Hawking visiting when
he experienced zero gravity?

ANSWERS

A1. Galileo Galilei.

A2. Bees.

A3. Trinity Hall, Cambridge University.

A4. Jane Wilde.

A5. Amyotrophic lateral sclerosis (ALS),
a form of Motor Neuron Disease.

A6. "Properties of Expanding Universes".

A7. Roger Penrose.

A8. First with a handheld clicker and then
via a cheek muscle attached to a sensor.

A9. 1988.

A10. The Kennedy Space Center.

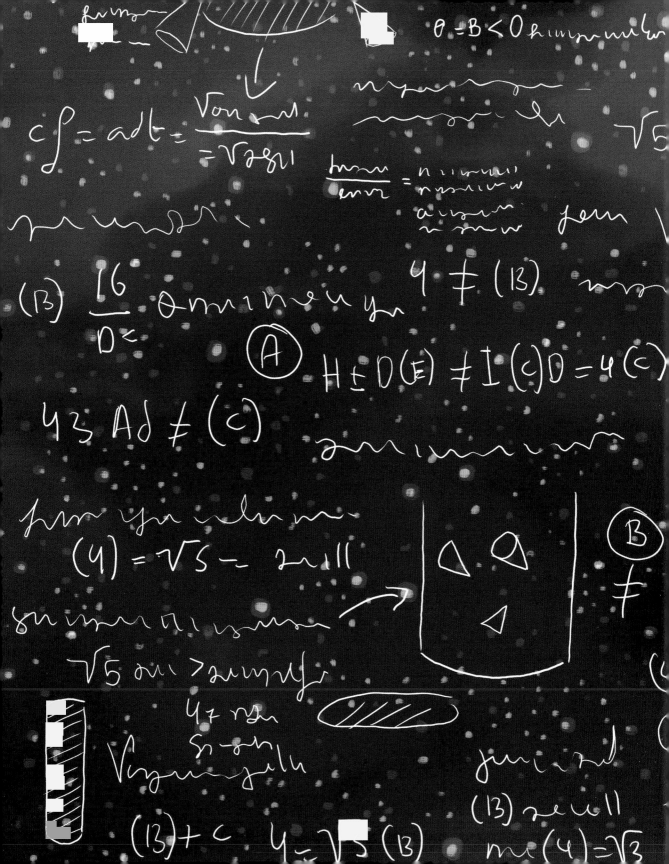